O'BRIEN **panda legends**

PANDA books are for young readers
making their own way
through books.

# O'BRIEN SERIES FOR YOUNG READERS

O'BRIEN panda legends

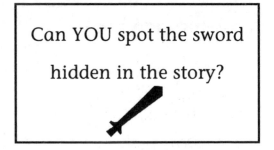

Can YOU spot the sword

hidden in the story?

# The Riddle

Retold by
FELICITY HAYES-MCCOY

Pictures by
• Randall Stephen Hall •

THE O'BRIEN PRESS
DUBLIN

First published 2008 by The O'Brien Press Ltd,
12 Terenure Road East, Dublin 6, Ireland.
Tel: +353 1 4923333; Fax: +353 1 4922777
E-mail: books@obrien.ie
Website: www.obrien.ie

ISBN: 978-1-84717-036-1

British Library Cataloguing-in-Publication Data
Hayes-McCoy, Felicity
The riddle. - (Panda tales)
1. Legends 2. Children's stories
I. Title  II. Hall, Randall Stephen
823.9'2[J]

The O'Brien Press receives assistance from

1  2  3  4  5  6  7  8  9  10
08  09  10  11  12  13  14

Typesetting, layout, editing, design: The O'Brien Press Ltd
Printed and bound in the UK by CPI Bookmarque, Croydon, CR0 4TD

# What's the
# Twist for Crookedness?

That's a riddle.

**Read the book
and find the answer.**

There was a man called
the **Gobán Saor**.
He was a
master craftsman.

There was nothing
he couldn't **make**
or **mend**.

There was nothing
he couldn't **build**
or **fix**.

Everyone wanted him
to work for them.

The Gobán Saor
lived with his wife
and his son in a house
in the middle of Ireland.

All sorts of people
came to his house
asking him to build
and to fix
and to make
and to mend for them.

The Prince of Spain
asked for a ship.

The Gobán Saor built it
with three masts and tall sails
and a golden bird at the front
and a silver fox at the back.

The Queen of Egypt wanted
a box for her jewels.

The Gobán Saor
made it out of wood,
with three secret drawers
and a hidden lock.

The man down the road
wanted him to fix a cart.

The Gobán Saor put
new wheels on it,
and a seat
with a leather cushion.

And he mended
the horse's harness too.

One day a messenger came
from the **King of Greece**.

'The King wants
the best palace in the world,'
said the messenger.
'And **you're** the man
to build it for him.'

The Gobán Saor
had just sat down
to read a book.

'What'll the King give me
if I build it?' he said.
'The crown off his head,'
said the messenger,
'and a bag of money.'

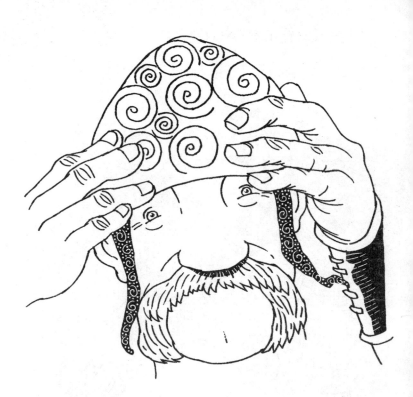

'Right,' said the Gobán Saor,
and he put on his hat.
'I'll finish my book
when I finish the palace.'

So he packed his tools
and kissed his wife.
And he and his son
set off.

They walked till
they came to the sea.
And there on the beach
was a speckled boat
waiting for them.

So they rowed away to Greece.

When they got there
the King had a
great welcome for them.

They had all the food
and drink they wanted
and soft beds to sleep in.

The Gobán Saor
built the palace.
And his son made
the tea.

And the King was always
coming and going,
telling them
how great they were.

They'd worked
for a year and a day
when the Gobán Saor
put down his hammer.

'That's it now,' he said,
'except for the very top
of the tallest tower.'

'That's great,' said his son.

'It is not,' said the Gobán Saor.

'**No**?' said the son.

'It's not,' said the Gobán Saor,
'because the King of Greece
has a plan.
He plans to **kill** me.'

'Why would he want
to do that?' said the son.

'Use your head,'
said the Gobán Saor.
'No good craftsman
ever stops learning.
Each job he does
is better than the last one.'

'This is the best palace
in the world **now**,'
said the Gobán Saor.

'But the next one I build
will be **better** still.
The King won't want that.'

The son thought about it.

'So he'll wait
till you've finished
this one,' he said,
'then he'll kill you
so you can't build
a better one.'

'That's his plan,'
said the Gobán Saor.

The son was scared.
But the Gobán Saor wasn't.

He called the King of Greece.
'What do you think
of your palace?' he said.

'It's the **best in the world**,'
said the King.

'I don't think so,'
said the Gobán Saor,
with a long face on him.

'It's **not**?' said the King.
'It isn't,' said the Gobán Saor.

'What's wrong
with it?'
said the King.

'I want **one tool**
to finish it,'
said the Gobán Saor,
'and I haven't got it.
It's at home
in my house
in the middle
of Ireland.'

Suddenly the King stopped
pretending to be nice.
He picked up the teapot
and threw it at the wall.

The Gobán Saor smiled.

'Do you know
what we'll do?' he said.
'We'll go home and get it.'
And he put on his hat.

'**You will not**,'
roared the King.
'You're going nowhere.'

'I'll send my **own son** for it,'
he said.

The Gobán Saor smiled.

'You're the boss,
so we'll do it
your way,' he said.
And he took his hat off.

'Tell your son
to ask my wife for
**The Twist for Crookedness**,'
said the Gobán Saor.
'She knows what that is.'

Then the King locked
the Gobán Saor and his son
in a room.
And he sent his own son
across the sea to Ireland.

When he got there
the King's son knocked
on the door.

The Gobán Saor's wife
opened it.

'The Gobán Saor
said to ask for the
**Twist For Crookedness**,'
said the King's son.
'Did he?' said the wife.
'Right,' she said. 'I know
what that is.'

She took him upstairs and
showed him a big box.
Then she opened the lid
and pointed inside.

'See if it's down there
at the bottom,' she said.

So the King's son
put his head in the box.
It was very dark.
And very deep.
He leaned right in
and reached right down.
But he couldn't feel the bottom.

Then the Gobán Saor's wife
grabbed his two feet
in her two hands ...
... and she tipped him in,

'That's the
**Twist for Crookedness**'
she said.

Then she slammed the lid.

And she turned the key.

And she went off, laughing.

Back in Greece,
the Gobán Saor and his son
were still locked up.

The son was scared.
But the Gobán Saor wasn't.

He was drawing plans
for his new garden shed.

A week passed.
And a month.
And another five minutes.

Up in his own room
the King was sitting
on his treasure chest.
He was cross.

He'd had time to think.
And now he knew
he'd been **tricked**.

He went to talk
to the Gobán Saor.

'I suppose I won't
see my son
till I let you go?'
said the King.

'I suppose you won't,'
said the Gobán Saor.

'Go on then, **go**,'
said the King.

'I'll go when
you've paid me,'
said the Gobán Saor.

He took the crown
off the King's head.
And he helped himself
from the treasure chest.

Then he and his son
walked down to the beach.

There was no
speckled boat
because the King's son
had taken it to Ireland.
But the Gobán Saor
made a raft out of shells.

He wore the crown.
And his son
sat on the money-bag.

And they floated home
in comfort.

When they came to the door
the Gobán Saor's wife
opened it.

'You're home,' she said.
'We are,' he said.

'I'll let out
your man above, so,'
she said.

She let out the King's son
and they gave him a big feed
of tea and rashers.
And they sent him
home to his Dad.

Then the Gobán Saor
sat down by the fire
with his book.

And he sent his son
outside to build
the garden shed.

No good craftsman
ever stops learning.
Each job he does
is better than the last one.

64